This book belongs to

. . . .

For the ~~mouse~~ TIGER in my house – K.N.
For the Foleys - the tigers of Leadhills – R.C.

First published 2019 by Macmillan Children's Books
an imprint of Pan Macmillan
This edition published 2021
The Smithson, 6 Briset Street, London EC1M 5NR
EU representative: Macmillan Publishers Ireland Limited,
Mallard Lodge, Lansdowne Village, Dublin 4
Associated companies throughout the world
www.panmacmillan.com

ISBN: 978-1-5290-8277-7

Text copyright © Karl Newson 2019
Illustration copyright © Ross Collins 2019

9 8 7 6 5 4 3 2 1

A CIP catalogue record for this book is
available from the British Library.

Printed in China

I AM A TIGER

KARL NEWSON   ROSS COLLINS

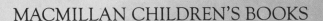

MACMILLAN CHILDREN'S BOOKS

I am a tiger.

No you're **not**!
A tiger is **much bigger**
than **you** are.

And it has a bit more
GRRRR!

Tigers can be
small, too.

GRRRr!

Not **that** small!
And a tiger has **stripes**.

Some do. This one
doesn't. So there.
I AM a tiger.

A **tiger** can climb a tree.
Can **you**?

I **could** climb a tree.
I could climb to the **moon**,
if I wanted to.
Most tigers can.

I AM a tiger.

Go on then!
Climb to the moon.

I can't just now.
It's time for my lunch.

A tiger **hunts** for its lunch.

GRRRR! I am a tiger.

No you're **not**!
You're a . . .

Ah . . .

AH CHOO!

I'm **not** an *Ah Ah Choo.*
I am a tiger.

Ha ha ha!
You're not a **tiger**.

You're a **mouse**!

Look at your **tiny, twitchy** nose.

Look at your **little** hands and feet.

I'll bet you had **cheese** for breakfast.

I AM a tiger.

I can do **this.**

Can you?

What about **this?**

Oh dear. **You**, Sir, are **definitely** a mouse.
And **I am a tiger**.

If **I** am a mouse,
then what are **they**?

Furry. Stripy.
Funny-looking face.

Long. Red.
Likes to bounce.

This is a caterpillar.

This is a balloon.

Thin. Pointy.
Hangs in trees.

Tiny. Colourful.
Sits on a stick.

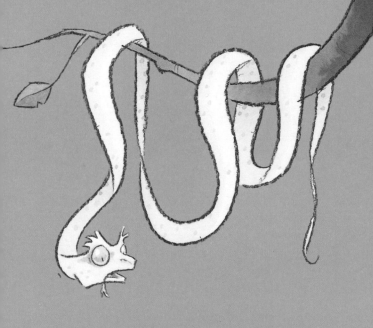

This is a banana.

This is a lollipop.

Now, I **really** must be going –
my lunch won't catch itself!

What a **silly** old bunch.

GAH! I am NOT a tiger!
How could I be so wrong!?

Look at those **teeth**.

Those **claws**.

That **tail**.

It's obvious . . .

I am a
CROCODILE!